D0376145

j

Avi
   Tom, Babette, & Simon:
Three Tales of Transformation

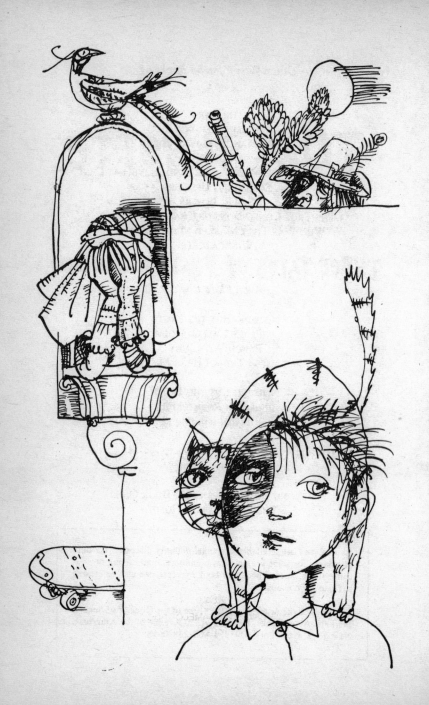

TOM, BABETTE, & SIMON

THREE TALES OF TRANSFORMATION

Avi

Illustrated by Alexi Natchev

AN AVON CAMELOT BOOK

AVON BOOKS
A division of
The Hearst Corporation
1350 Avenue of the Americas
New York, New York 10019

Copyright © 1995 by Avi
Interior illustrations copyright © 1995 by Alexi Natchev
Published by arrangement with Macmillan Books for Young Readers
Visit our website at **http://AvonBooks.com**
Library of Congress Catalog Card Number: 94-35195
ISBN: 0-380-72770-6
RL: 4.4

First Avon Camelot Printing: August 1997

CAMELOT TRADEMARK REG. U.S. PAT. OFF. AND IN OTHER COUNTRIES, MARCA REGISTRADA,
HECHO EN U.S.A.

Printed in the U.S.A.

OPM 10 9 8 7 6 5 4 3 2 1

These three tales are for my three nieces

Nicole
Diane
Jean

TOM

At the age of twelve Thomas Osborn Pitz—better known as Tom—had few interests, little desire, and almost no energy. This was so despite a family—mother, father, older brother, and sister—who loved him. As for school, his teachers treated him fairly, he did the things he was supposed to do, and he received passable grades. But if you were to ask Tom what the future held for him, he would have replied that, other than getting older, he expected no change. In short, Thomas Osborn Pitz—better known as Tom—found life boring.

One day when Tom was doing what he did most often, that is, sitting on the front steps of his city house doing nothing, a shorthaired, black-and-white cat with gray eyes approached and sat down before him. For a while the two—boy and cat—stared at one another.

It was the cat who spoke first. "What's happening?" he asked.

"Not much," Tom replied.

"Doing anything?" the cat asked.

"Nope."

"Just hanging out?"

"I guess."

"That something you do often?"

"Yeah."

"How come?" the cat inquired.

"I'm bored."

The cat considered this remark carefully and then said, "You look like my kind of friend. How about adopting me?"

"Why should I?"

"Got anything better to do?"

"Nope."

"Well, then?"

Tom asked, "What's your name?"

To which the cat replied, "Charley."

So it was that Tom took Charley in. Moreover the cat became part of the household. So familiar did he become that when Tom went to sleep, Charley slept right next to Tom's head on an extra pillow. Indeed, from that time on that was how the two—boy and cat—spent their nights.

"Hey, man," Tom said to Charley one afternoon two months after the cat had moved in. "You get to sleep all day, but I have to go to school." In disgust he flung his schoolbooks onto his bed.

It was the statement more than the thump of books that woke Charley from a sound nap. He studied Tom, then stretched his back. "I am a cat," he said. "You are a boy. Some would say you had it better."

Tom sighed. "If you had to go to school every day like I do, you wouldn't believe that."

"Don't you like school?" Charley asked with a look and tone of sympathy.

3

"Oh, I like it all right," Tom replied. "The kids are okay. The teachers are all right. Once in a while it even gets almost interesting. But mostly it's just boring. Actually, I'd rather do nothing. Like you."

"What about life beyond school?"

"Bor-ing," Tom insisted.

"Doesn't *anything* interest you?"

Tom considered the question. "Television," he said at last. "At least on TV there's something happening. It's my life that's dull."

With great care, Charley said, "A cat's life—or mine anyway—can be a bit dull, too."

"Your life isn't supposed to be anything but dull," Tom said with envy. "But people are *always* telling me that I should get up and *do* something. Boy, wish I had permission to sleep all day the way you do."

To which Charley said, "How about if you became me, a cat, and I became you, a boy?"

"Not possible," Tom said with a wistful shrug.

"Oh, I don't know," Charley said. "Most people wouldn't believe that you and I could hold a conversation, but here we are doing exactly that."

"To tell you the truth," Tom said, "it's not that interesting a conversation."

"Whatever you say," Charley replied as he curled himself into a ball, closed his eyes, and went back to sleep. Tom, feeling envious, did the next best thing. He went and watched television.

Next day Tom, as usual, went to school. In most ways it was ordinary. Although Ms. Donnigan did call upon him once and he gave a reasonable response, he never raised his hand. Most of the time he doodled, stared out the window, and daydreamed, but about what he could not have said.

At the end of the day, however, Ms. Donnigan announced a special homework assignment. She asked each student to write an essay titled "The Most Exciting Thing that Ever Happened to Me." It was due in one week's time.

All Tom could think was, "Bor-ing."

As he walked home Tom struggled to recall the most exciting thing that had happened to him. He did remember a time during a family trip when they had a flat tire on the highway. That, however, was not so much exciting as it was nerve-racking.

Then there was the time he was taken to a baseball game, but no one got so much as one hit until the ninth inning.

Tom also recalled the time his mother thought she might lose her job. That was scary, though, not exciting.

"You ever do anything exciting in your life?" Tom asked Charley when he got home.

Charley, who had been sleeping on Tom's bed, woke at the sound of Tom's voice. He stretched, yawned, and said, "As a cat?"

"Of course as a cat."

Charley said, "I caught a mouse once."

"Was that exciting?"

"It was only a small mouse. The first I ever got."

"What did you do with it?"

"Let it go."

"Anything else?"

"Since I've moved in here I've caught a whiff of another cat passing through your backyard. I believe it's a cat of my acquaintance—Peggy is her name—who's in search of a home of her own."

"Is *that* exciting?"

"For a cat, it is," Charley admitted. "Why all these questions?"

Tom told Charley about the essay he had to write. "But," he complained, "nothing exciting has *ever* happened to me."

Charley pondered Tom's words with care. "Tom," he said at last, "do you remember what I told you, that you could become me, and I could become you?"

"Yeah."

"You might find *that* exciting."

Tom sighed. "Right," he said. "Sleeping all day with no one objecting does sound cool. Could it really be done?"

"We can give it a shot," Charley said. "A few blocks from here there's a neighborhood wizard cat. We could ask her."

"If we make the change," Tom warned, "you'd have to write that essay. It's due next week."

"I suppose. But, as you suggested, you'd get to sleep all day."

"Sounds okay to me," Tom admitted. "Anyway, we

could do it just long enough for you to write my essay."

"Well then," Charley offered, "how about making the change now?"

"*Now?*" Tom exclaimed. He was not given to making quick decisions.

"Any reason not to?"

When Tom could not think of any, they left at once.

It was dusk. A thin haze filled the air. Even as they walked streetlamps began to flicker on. People on the street moved swiftly as if eager to get inside. Tom was glad Charley knew the way.

They went two blocks to the right, one to the left, then cut through a back alley Tom had never wanted to pass through. Next they navigated a weed-and bedspring-infested yard, then approached what looked to Tom to be an abandoned apartment building. All its windows were boarded up. Tom hoped they would not be going there. Charley, however, without so much as a pause, padded into the building's basement and down a long empty corridor. Tom began to feel nervous.

"We have far to go?" he asked.

"Hang in there," Charley replied as he headed up a flight of steps.

They reached the first floor. It took a while for Tom's eyes to grow accustomed to the gloom, but when they did Tom realized that the building was full of cats. Some were sleeping. Others sat with tails curled about their feet staring into the distance. A few prowled restlessly. Charley nodded to a few as if they were acquaintances.

With Charley still leading, Tom entered a long and dimly lit hallway which had green paint peeling from the walls and a ceiling that looked like it might fall any moment. Here were more cats. While some glanced at Tom, most paid no attention.

At the end of the hallway was a door. Before this door stood a large cat, quite the largest cat Tom had ever seen. Weighing at least twenty pounds, he looked like a miniature tiger.

Charley approached the large cat with care and respect. For a few moments the two cats stared at each other, their tails moving restlessly.

"What can we do for you?" the large cat eventually asked.

"A transformation," Charley said.

Tom saw the large cat's eyes shift to him, then flick back to Charley. "Any particular reason?" the large cat asked.

"He's bored," Charley replied. "And he has to write a school essay, 'The Most Exciting Thing that Ever Happened to Me.'"

"Oh, one of *those*," the large cat said as if he had heard it all before. "You can enter," he said and opened the door.

"Watch your head," Charley cautioned.

Tom was just about to ask Charley if this kind of transformation was often made when they stepped into a small dark room. Here, the floor was so carpeted with cats it was hard to move about. Some cats were big, others small. Some were perched on ledges. Others sat on shelves like so many books in a library. The whole room throbbed with the steady sound of purring, as if one low note on a bass guitar was being continually thrummed.

No matter where the cats sat or lay, all eyes were

fixed upon a raised platform at the far end of the room. This platform was illuminated by a shaft of pale yellow sunlight that cut through a broken piece of window boarding.

On the platform a not-very-large cat lay stretched full-length upon a purple pillow. Her eyes were closed to narrow slits. One cheek rested on an extended front leg. Save for the tip of her tail, which now and again shivered delicately, she lay perfectly still. Her long silver hair made it appear as if she were dressed in silken lounging pajamas.

"Who's that?" Tom whispered to Charley.

"Her name is Peggy," Charley whispered.

Tom had a vague memory that he had heard the name before. Before he could think it through, Charley said, "On the streets she leads a normal life. Here, however, she's the local cat wizard. That's not unusual. Lots of neighborhoods have them.

"Now, just follow me, and don't say a thing unless you're asked a direct question."

"I hear you."

Charley maneuvered his way close to the platform. Once there, he lay down and tucked his front paws under his chest. "Kneel," he whispered. Tom knelt.

"Now, be patient."

Tom gazed at Peggy with interest, curious how such a cat became a wizard. Then he began to think about what Charley had said, that she led a regular street life.

Suddenly Peggy looked up. "What's happening?" she asked in a small, almost delicate voice.

"Peg," Charley said, "we're requesting a transformation. This boy—his name is Tom—and myself."

"Wants to be a regular tomcat, I suppose," Peggy said. Her silky sides rippled slightly as she enjoyed her little joke.

"Actually," Charley explained, "he's bored. Wants a license to sleep all day, the way I do."

"Lucky you," Peggy murmured to Charley. With a sidelong glance at Tom, she asked, "Do you want to sleep all day?"

It took a moment for Tom to realize he was being spoken to.

"Oh yes, ma'am," Tom replied. "I love to sleep."

12

Peggy sighed. "I'd settle for a decent home off the streets."

"We've got that," Tom said quickly.

"Whatever you say," Peggy mumbled with a slight rise of her left eyebrow. "Bow down," she said. "I need your heads close together."

Tom bowed as Charley did the same, so that their heads were side by side.

Tom was not precisely sure what happened next. What he sensed was that Peggy's tail curled around and batted him on the forehead. He supposed the same thing happened to Charley. The next thing he heard Peggy say was, "Charley, enjoy that home of yours."

"Let's go," Charley said. Tom turned. Right away he felt as if the room had grown much larger. What's more he was staring—nose to nose—into the face of an enormous calico cat with great curled whiskers. "Beg pardon," Tom said, and took a side step.

He turned to see if Charley was there. What he saw was the leg of the largest human being he had ever seen, a creature who towered high into the room, so high Tom could not see his head.

Momentarily confused, Tom called, "Charley?"

"Right here," came a voice as big as heaven itself.

Something like a shock ran through Tom from the tip of his nose leather to the tip of his tail. And indeed, he had a tail because he'd become a cat. Not just any cat, either, but one who looked exactly like Charley, even as Charley now looked exactly like Tom.

Tom lifted a hand before his face. It was a paw and was covered with black-and-white fur. "Too cool," he said to himself. "I've become a cat—like Charley."

"Let's go," Charley urged and gave Tom a gentle spank to get him out the door.

Though Tom had spent his life living in that neighborhood, going home was like traveling through a foreign land. Everything was gigantic. Even things he could recognize—like mailboxes—appeared to be twisted into odd shapes.

What's more, he seemed to be at the bottom of a sea of smells. One moment he sensed something delicious to eat. The next moment he had a trembling

awareness of danger that was almost instantly followed by a whiff of calm. That in turn was taken over by the delicate scent of friendship. Tom, who had never been aware of such smells, was astonished he could identify them so clearly.

Even more amazing was that his own body felt so different. He had never thought much about having hands and feet, or even a head, save when he bumped them or they hurt. Now he felt all loose and jangly, as though he was not tied together tightly. Then too, he was acutely aware of his own skin. Not only did some spots feel dirty, he had a deep desire to lick them clean. Other places itched and were in need of scratching. He even had the inclination to fling himself down, stretch out, and flex his nails into something deep and nice, like a soft stuffed chair.

The reason he resisted doing all these things was because he was having trouble keeping up with Charley. Charley—the boy—was striding along on long human legs in a purposeful manner.

"Come on, don't dawdle," Charley kept saying. Tom, fearing he would never get back home on his own, loped along.

16

They reached their house. Tom was about to open the door when he realized he could no longer manage it. Charley had to do it.

"Oh, there you are," came the familiar voice of Tom's father. "I was wondering where you went."

Tom answered. "Charley and I went for a walk," he said, but the only sound he heard was a meow.

"That cat seems to know," Tom's father said with a good-natured laugh. "Where were you?"

"Just hanging around the neighborhood," Charley said vaguely.

"Don't you have homework to do?"

"No problem. I just have to start writing an essay called 'The Most Exciting Thing that Ever Happened to Me.' "

"Interesting. What are you going to write about?"

"Don't know. But I'm really looking forward to it."

"Hey, love to hear that enthusiasm for a change!" Tom's father exclaimed.

Tom, curling about Charley's feet, suddenly felt contented. "I'm going off to sleep," he announced. Charley reached down and gave Tom a reassuring scratch behind the ear.

Tom strolled over to his own bed, leaped up, found the cat's pillow, and closed his eyes in perfect pleasure. In moments he was asleep, purring gently. Charley, meanwhile, set about composing the essay.

During the next few days all went well. Tom truly enjoyed doing nothing, sleeping all day atop the pillow on his own bed. Now and again he slept in different places about the apartment, and once he went for a stroll in the backyard. Generally speaking, however, he did nothing but stay on his bed and sleep.

Over the same period Charley lived Tom's life. He went to school. He made friends. He enjoyed Tom's family.

It was on the fifth day that Tom began to get a little restless. The truth was he was becoming bored with sleep. He would have watched television but he would have had to wait for others to turn it on, and they didn't always choose his programs.

Twice Tom actually started to read the daily newspapers only to be picked up and placed firmly in the litter box.

At last he ventured onto the streets. There he narrowly avoided being hit by a car, had his tail pulled by an infant, was teased by an older child, then chased home by a dog. He began to think he'd had enough of being a cat.

That afternoon, when Charley came home from school, he flung his schoolbooks down and said to Tom, "Today was not a good day!"

Tom woke, yawned, stretched, and looked around. "What's the matter?" he asked.

"Remember that essay?"

" 'The Most Exciting Thing that Ever Happened to Me?' "

"Exactly," Charley said. "It was due today and you know how hard I worked on it. When we got to the moment to share papers, I volunteered to read mine."

"Ms. Donnigan must have been surprised."

"She certainly was. Apparently you never volunteered anything."

"Not me," Tom agreed.

"Anyway, she called on me and I read."

"What happened?"

Charley held up the pages he had written. "She said my work was a fine piece of writing but she didn't want fiction. She wanted something *real*."

"What did you write about?"

"Transformations. How I, once a boy, became a cat. Every word of it was true. But she didn't believe it, though she admitted it was enjoyable. The class liked it, too. But I have to do the whole thing again." In disgust, Charley threw the papers down.

Tom scratched himself beneath the chin. "You could write about that time you caught a mouse."

"She wouldn't believe that either," Charley said and went off in a huff.

Tom, reminding himself that he wanted to talk to Charley about going through a retransformation process, was just about to go back to sleep when something the boy had said floated through his mind. What was it? Oh, yes . . . did Charley say that the subject he had written about was "How I, once a boy, became a cat"?

Tom grinned. Surely what Charley meant to say was the other way around: That is, "How I, once a cat, became a boy." Or was he writing about how he, Tom, became a cat?

It was a bit confusing, so Tom shut his eyes again.

But he could not sleep. He was too bothered by what Charley had said.

At last he got up and looked around, meaning to speak to Charley. Charley, however, had gone out. Then Tom noticed that the paper Charley had written was lying on the table.

He read it. It was exactly what Charley had said it was, a report about a boy who had turned into a cat. This boy, so Charley had written, wished to become a cat and sleep all the time. That was familiar enough. In fact, as Tom went through it, the whole story was pretty much like his own experience. However, in Charley's story, the boy's name was Charley and the cat's name was Felix.

Why, Tom wondered, would Charley have everything the same, *except* the names? He decided to find out.

"Hey, Charley," Tom said that night as Charley sat at Tom's desk working on his new essay. "I read your essay."

Charley glanced around. He seemed taken aback. "You did?"

"You left it around."

"Oh, right. Did you . . . like it?"

"It was fine," said Tom. "It was all accurate, too. Except for one, or actually two, things."

"What was that?"

"You changed the names around. You called the boy Charley and the cat Felix."

"That so?" Charley said evasively, turning back to his work.

"How come you did that?" Tom persisted.

"It was supposed to be true," Charley explained.

Tom frowned. "I don't follow."

This time Charley turned around to gaze at Tom evenly. "I guess there's no harm in your knowing *now*."

"Knowing what, *now*?"

"Well, before I introduced myself to you and you took me in, I was once a boy, and my name was Charles."

"You *were*?"

"Yup. See, I was really bored with my life. So bored I began thinking that things would be better if I were a cat. As it turned out, I met a cat. Or rather, this cat introduced himself to me. His name was

Felix. Felix knew about one of these neighborhood cat wizards. Sound familiar? You can guess the rest."

As Charley told this story, Tom felt more and more uncomfortable. At last he said, "Charley, do you mean to say that as you sit at *my* desk, wearing *my* clothes, doing *my* homework, looking like *me*—that at one time *you* were a boy and then *became* a cat? But then you decided you didn't want to be a cat and so became me instead?"

"You've got it."

"But . . . but why didn't you and that Felix just change back to what you were?"

"He didn't want to be a cat again."

"He didn't?"

"Nope."

Tom took a moment to think this through. Then he said, "So you found me, and tricked me into—"

Tom did not even finish the sentence before Charley said, "Yes."

"But that's outrageous!" Tom cried. "Anyway," he said, "I've had enough of sleeping. I want to change back."

"Sorry," Charley said brusquely. "Too late for that."

Tom, who was getting increasingly upset, stared at Charley. "What do you mean?"

"I much prefer being a boy again. Besides, this is a great place and I like your family. They're nice." So saying, he left the room, shutting the door behind him.

At first Tom was too astounded to do anything. Then he leaped off the bed and headed right for the door, only to remember that he had to get a person to open it for him. He called to Charley, but it was not Charley who came. It was his mother.

"Want to go out?" she asked, reaching down and chucking Tom under the chin.

"Of course I want to go out," Tom said in a rather irritated way. But when he spoke to his mother, all she heard was caterwauling.

"Isn't it cute the way cats talk," she said as she gathered him up and set him gently but firmly out the front door. "Now go play," she said.

An indignant Tom looked up and down the street, trying to orient himself. It all looked so very different now that he was a cat. He closed his eyes and breathed in, trying to sort out the many scents. Then he began to go toward what he hoped would be an audience with Peggy.

It took a while but Tom found the abandoned building. Once again he went into the basement, then up the steps to the long dimly lit hallway, passing through the multitude of cats. Again, before the doorway at the end of the hall, stood the large cat.

"What can we do for you?" the large cat demanded.

Tom said, "A transformation."

The large cat sniffed. "With whom?"

"With the one I was transformed from."

"Is he here?"

"Well, no."

"Forget it. Anyway, Peggy's out."

"Where?"

"Hey, pal, she has her own life to take care of."

"But . . ."

"Beat it kit-cat," snarled the large cat, and he hissed. Tom backed away and made his way home.

That night Tom had it out with Charley. "The

25

point is," Tom said hotly, "you weren't being honest with me. In your paper you said you were a boy."

"I was."

"Then you became a cat, and now you're a boy again."

"Right."

"And you say you have no desire to change back."

"I'm being honest there," Charley said. "As for you, you wanted to sleep all day, didn't you? To do nothing but lie about."

"Yeah. Right. But I've done that, and it's even more boring than staying awake."

"Tom, you made the deal. If you don't like it, go find another kid who is as bored with things as you were. Believe me, there are plenty of them. A lot of the cats at Peggy's used to be kids who were bored with their lives."

"That's not true!"

"Hey, half the kids in your class used to be cats!"

Tom was shocked. "They did?"

"Absolutely," Charley insisted. "You know, kids get bored. Want to sleep. Bingo! Become cats. Cats become kids. They're usually the lively ones."

"But I *want* to be a human again," Tom cried, "not some cat!"

"Too late for that! Now, please leave me in peace. I still have to write this essay."

"But . . ."

Suddenly Charley scooped Tom up, and despite Tom's howl of protest, put him out of the room.

Tom slipped out of the house through an open window. It was quite late, and the moon was large in the sky. He went around to the backyard, climbed the fence, and sniffed. The air was full of pungent smells. But the only smell he found interesting was the scent of his own home. It made his heart ache. Lifting his head, he let out a long piercing howl of misery. Then another.

A window opened. A voice growled, "Shut up, cat! I'm trying to sleep!"

It was a mournful Tom who slunk out of the yard and onto the streets. A thousand distinct odors wafted through the air, a tapestry of smells, far too complex for Tom to untangle.

He wandered on, paying little heed to where he

was going, up and down streets, through alleys, along back fences.

He had been walking for about an hour when he heard a great spitting and hissing. He stopped and listened. It was a cat fight. He looked to see where it was coming from, spied an alley, and trotted over.

At the far end of the alley he could make out two cats. One was large, the other a small silver gray. The small one had been forced back against the alley fence by the larger one. The large one was yowling, preparing to attack.

"Help!" cried the gray cat. "Help!"

Hardly thinking of what he was doing, Tom let out a howl of his own and dashed down the alley. The large cat turned to confront him. Tom was too quick. In one bound he leaped over the large cat and came down beside the smaller one. There Tom hissed, showing his teeth and raising a claw-extended paw.

The big cat, now confronted by two cats, backed off, turned, and fled.

"He's gone," Tom said, panting to catch his breath.

"Oh, thank you," the gray cat replied.

Tom turned and looked at this other cat for the first time. "Hey, you're Peggy, the wizard cat!" he cried.

"Do I know you?" Peggy said.

"My name is Tom. You transformed me from a boy. The cat was named Charley."

"Oh, dear, I'm afraid I can't remember. These cases come in litters. After a while all you people look alike."

"We do?"

"A certain blandness. No show of emotion. As if you can't bother. You make perfect cats. So, sorry, I don't remember you. But I am ever so grateful. If I can ever return the favor . . ."

"Oh, but you can," Tom said eagerly.

"How's that?"

"Transform me back."

"To what you were?"

"Absolutely."

"How does the other one—the one I transformed you with—feel?"

"I don't think he wants to switch."

"That's the usual case. It makes things almost impossible."

"But you can do it, can't you?"

"Oh sure, but the point is, you have to get the two heads side by side. If one doesn't want to, and that one is a human, well, like I say, it isn't easy."

"I can arrange that!" Tom cried.

"How?"

"Follow me."

Tom led the way back to his own house. They reached it by two in the morning. Finding the window through which Tom got out still open, they crawled inside.

Peggy looked about. "Nice place you got here," she muttered.

"Shh," Tom cautioned.

He made his way to his room, and by standing up on his hind legs—Peggy helped here—they were able to push the door open.

Charley lay fast asleep on the bed, his head upon the pillow.

"Now listen carefully," Tom whispered to Peggy. "I'll get on the pillow right next to him and put my head near his. Give me a minute. Then, you jump on and do what you normally do. Just make the transformation."

Peggy giggled. "Someone's going to be surprised when he wakes up."

"That's his problem. He tricked me into this."

Peggy sniffed. "That's what you all say."

Not wishing to argue, Tom leaped onto the bed and padded softly to his own pillow. Once there he lay down, tucked his paws under his chest, and set his head right next to Charley's head.

Within moments Peggy followed. "Ready?" she asked in a small voice.

"Ready," Tom replied.

"Here goes," Peggy warned.

Tom closed his eyes, and waited for the tap on his forehead. When nothing happened he opened his eyes and found himself staring right into the face of a gray cat.

Puzzled, Tom called, "Peggy?"

"The name's Charley," the cat said.

"Charley?" Tom cried and looked down at himself. He was just the way he had been moments before—a cat. In a panic, he turned. There asleep was a person who looked exactly like he used to look. As for the second cat, it looked just like Peggy.

"Hey," Charley—now Peggy—growled, "what's going on? How come I'm a cat again?"

"It's Peggy," stammered Tom.

"Peggy? The cat wizard?"

"I'm afraid so. She did the transformation on herself and you. She's become us."

One week later Tom—who had spent all his time prowling the streets—suddenly stopped. He was in a park not far from a bench. Sitting on the bench was a girl. She wasn't doing anything in particular, just sitting. Now and again she swung a leg back and forth. Then she yawned, looked at her watch, and yawned again.

Tom watched her for about fifteen minutes. In all that time the girl continued to just sit there, a slight frown upon her face. She looked bored.

Casually, Tom approached. He sat down in front of the girl.

"What's happening?" he said.

The girl looked up at him. After a moment she said, "Nothing."

Tom asked, "Doing anything?"

"Nothing *to* do," the girl replied sulkily.

Smiling, Tom got up, stretched, then rubbed himself against her leg. "You sound like my kind of friend," he said. "How about adopting me?"

BABETTE

In the ancient country of Solandia, there lived a certain Queen Isabelle and her husband, King Alfredo.

In Solandia it was a queen, not a king, who ruled the country. If the reigning royal couple's firstborn was not a daughter, the crown would pass to the firstborn daughter of the queen's sister or, if necessary, to her eldest female cousin's firstborn daughter.

Quite naturally, then, Queen Isabelle wished to give birth to a girl so that her daughter would become queen. Furthermore, since the queen considered herself a beautiful woman, she believed only beautiful girls could be happy. It was hardly a surprise then that she was insistent that any daughter of hers *must* be beautiful.

To insist upon these things was all very well, but since the queen knew of no way to insure she would have a daughter—and a beautiful daughter at that—the queen and king had *no* child at all.

Even so, a beautiful daughter was all Queen Isabelle thought about. If you asked—or even if you did not—the queen could—and would—tell you what this hoped-for daughter would look like. What's more, she could—*and would*—describe her beauty in great detail for hours at a time. She even knew her name: Babette.

And yet there was no child.

One day a lady-in-waiting told Queen Isabelle about rumors regarding a woman named Esmeralda, who had recently arrived in the city. This Esmeralda—so it was said—had powers that would allow a woman to have exactly the kind of child she desired. The lady-in-waiting even told the queen where this Esmeralda lived.

"What nonsense!" the queen exclaimed, dismissing the lady-in-waiting with a wave of her hand. Nonetheless, as soon as she was alone, the queen disguised herself and made her way to a dank corner of the city where she had never been before. There she knocked upon an ancient door.

The knock was answered by an old woman with a thin and twisted body. Her face was haggard. Her hair was gray. Her hands were gnarled and ribboned with veins. A tattered blue-and-green shawl lay upon her frail shoulders.

The queen, shocked by the appearance of someone she considered very ugly, stepped back from the door. "I think I have made a mistake," she said hastily, turning to go.

But before the queen could go three steps, the old woman cried, "O, my queen, I am Esmeralda, the only person who can help you have the beautiful daughter you so desire!"

Queen Isabelle stopped and looked back at the woman in amazement. "How do you know who I am and what I wish?" she demanded.

In a voice thick with accent, Esmeralda said, "Because my powers are mirrors that reflect your desires."

The queen considered this. "How can you, who are so ugly, help me get a beautiful daughter?"

Esmeralda, in an effort to ignore the cruel remark, smiled crookedly and said, "Trust me."

The queen laughed with scorn. "Do you really expect me to trust someone I don't desire to look at?"

These words made Esmeralda's eyes gleam with anger. All she said, however, was, "My queen, I have a mirror which I will place between us. Then you can talk to me but only look upon yourself."

Though the queen was torn between wanting the daughter of her dreams and being revolted by Esmeralda's appearance, it was her desire for the beautiful daughter that proved stronger. "Very well," she said. "I will let you help me." With that she entered the old woman's hovel.

Esmeralda placed a large mirror in the very center of her small room. This mirror was taller than it was wide—like a door—and framed by wood that had been intricately carved. The carvings were of forest animals and birds, as well as flowers, all crafted so well they seemed to be alive. The mirror's surface shimmered and sparkled.

While Esmeralda sat on one side of the mirror, the queen sat on the other, so that the queen gazed only at her own image. Though she had always considered herself beautiful, in this mirror the queen saw herself as an image of perfection. This pleased her greatly and she began to relax.

"Very well," Esmeralda called out from behind the mirror, "tell me about the daughter of your desires."

As always, Queen Isabelle found it impossible to resist talking about her would-be daughter. "Babette must be a beautiful girl," the queen began. "A child without so much as one blemish or irregularity."

"Why must she be beautiful?"

To which the queen replied, "The whole world knows only the beautiful are happy."

"Ah," Esmeralda said, "you wish her to be . . . what is the word?"

"*Flawless,*" the queen prompted.

"Excellent!" said Esmeralda. "My powers can reflect that."

"Then use them," Queen Isabelle commanded.

"It shall be so!" Esmeralda cried with glee.

So saying, the old woman placed one of her hands on the top of the mirror and her other hand on the bottom. Then she began to squeeze. Instead of shattering, the mirror collapsed into a glassy lump. Esmeralda then squeezed this lump until it became smaller and smaller. When the lump became perfectly round and no bigger than the tip of her small finger, she pressed it inside out with her thumbs, until it became invisible. This invisible pill she placed in the queen's hand.

"Swallow this," Esmeralda said, "and I promise you shall have a daughter who will appear flawless."

For a moment Queen Isabelle paused. Then she recalled that the pill was made from the very mirror which had made *her* look so beautiful. So she swallowed the invisible pill and waited for something to happen. Nothing did. Annoyed, she jumped up. "I suppose you now wish me to pay you for something I cannot even see?"

"My queen," Esmeralda replied with a bow deep enough to hide the glint in her eye. "Who am I to ask anything from such a beautiful and gracious queen? I am more than content in thinking that I've been able to make you happier than you already are by helping you have a flawless daughter."

Queen Isabelle was pleased by such a show of humility. She flung a halfpenny at the woman's feet and hurried away.

As the queen hastened home, however, she began to grow uneasy about this Esmeralda and what had happened. Perhaps the ugly woman had been insincere in her parting words. Perhaps she would talk about the queen's secret visit. Perhaps she would mock her. Who knew what claims the woman might make?

By the time the queen had returned home she decided it would be better to banish the woman to the farthest corner of the country. It was done immediately.

Now, at first Queen Isabelle doubted whether her visit—and the invisible pill—had been worth her while. Yet not very long after, the queen announced with great joy that she was going to have a baby.

When the baby was born it was indeed a girl. What's more, she was normal in all respects save for one thing: she was *invisible*.

The moment the child was born, the hardworking and distracted midwife automatically wrapped the baby up in a sweet smelling blanket, then handed the precious bundle to her mother, the queen. With great eagerness the queen pulled aside the blankets and peeked at her baby's face. For a brief moment— a very, *very* brief moment—Queen Isabelle saw nothing. But it was quite impossible for her to believe she had given birth to *nothing*. Besides, the bundle had a lusty voice, it smelled like a baby, and it moved like a baby. Certainly the bundle showed the appetite of a baby. Best of all, the child was without one noticeable blemish!

So after one brief heart-stopping moment when Queen Isabelle saw nothing, the very *next* second she was convinced she was looking at the most beautiful baby girl, named Babette—the very child she had long imagined and always wanted.

With Babette secure in her mother's arms, the

midwife stepped outside the delivery room where King Alfredo was waiting anxiously.

"How is my wife?" he asked.

"Everything went splendidly," the midwife replied.

"Wonderful! And the child?"

"A girl. A perfect child."

"Even better! May I see them?"

Instead of answering, the midwife led the king to the queen's bedside. There the queen said, "Here, husband of mine, is Babette, our new daughter. Isn't she every bit as beautiful as I desired?"

The king peeked inside the bundle. For just the very small part of a very small second, he saw nothing.

"Not so much as one blemish, has she?" said Queen Isabelle.

The king hesitated but felt compelled to agree. Then he said, "What do you like most about her?"

"Exactly what I expected to like," the queen told him. "Her clear blue eyes and blond hair. So like my mother's."

King Alfredo looked again and this time—in his

mind's eye—he saw the beautiful daughter his wife had so often and vividly described. So he said, "Yes, her eyes *are* splendid." Then he added, "But, I confess, it's her delicate nose, and noble forehead—which she gets from my side of the family—that *I* admire!"

"How perceptive you are," the queen said.

Since the birth of Princess Babette was important news in the Queendom of Solandia, the king went to the prime minister and told that wise gentleman how well everything had gone.

"Is the princess as perfect as her mother desired?" the prime minister inquired. He was not prime minister for nothing.

"The girl is flawless," King Alfredo replied. "Just what was wanted!" And he described Babette in great detail.

The prime minister went to the lord high information officer and told *him* the happy news.

"We must send out a proclamation at once," the lord high information officer said. "With," he added, "an appropriate portrait of the princess!"

The prime minister agreed.

"Of course," the lord high information officer said, "to do so I must know what Princess Babette looks like."

The prime minister hastily provided him with the king's description, adding some details from what he recalled of the way Queen Isabelle had spoken of the much desired child.

The lord high information officer went to the royal court artist and asked him to do a portrait of the new princess so every citizen in Solandia would know her likeness.

"Can you describe her to me?" the royal court artist asked.

"Of course!" the lord high information officer said, providing a fine verbal portrait of Babette—just as *he* had been told.

The royal court artist—who was famous not only for his artistic skill but even more for his ability to create art that satisfied his clients' high ideals— made the portrait. Since there was no one he wished to satisfy more than Queen Isabelle, he painted a picture of the new princess exactly as the queen had described her.

Very soon thereafter, a royal proclamation, complete with a lovely portrait of beautiful Princess Babette, was printed and distributed to every person in Solandia. The citizens, seeing the sweet face of the new princess, their future queen, were enormously proud. How satisfying that their nation had a princess without so much as one blemish! Long live Solandia!

Of course, when the people actually saw Princess Babette, they did experience a puzzling moment. Still, all they had to do was glance at the proclamation portrait to tell them *exactly* what Babette looked like. Then they were doubly pleased because the image they saw was indeed perfect.

There was one other thing that occurred shortly after Babette's birth. The queen proclaimed a new law. It was a law that banished all mirrors from the Queendom of Solandia.

Alas, before Babette was one year old, Queen Isabelle and King Alfredo died. The queen's death came from madness. Her first symptoms appeared when she took to avoiding all light, and insisted upon sitting in dark rooms. Next she bound up her eyes and walked about like a blind person. Her actual death came during the night, when she accidentally fell from the highest point of the castle. "She could not see where she was going," it was whispered.

As for King Alfredo's death, though the doctors gave medical reasons, it was commonly understood that he died of grief over the loss of his beloved wife. Indeed, his last words were, "I can no longer see any reason to live."

When these sad events transpired, Princess Babette, not yet one year of age, was far too young to take the throne. One needed to be at least sixteen. The queendom was ruled—quite properly, it must be said—by the prime minister on her behalf.

Now, although Babette remained invisible, and despite the fact that mirrors were banned from the queendom, the young princess knew exactly what she looked like. She knew by looking at portraits of herself. These pictures were placed throughout the palace on every wall of every room.

Indeed, the prime minister decreed that a portrait of the princess be placed in every home throughout Solandia.

As for the artists of Solandia, they loved to paint her picture, readily confessing that Babette was—after all—the perfect subject.

Did Babette look the same in every portrait? Of course not. Since the talents of the many artists differed, the images differed. Still, certain qualities were there. Babette was always beautiful. She never had a blemish. She was perfect.

Many years passed. As Babette approached her sixteenth birthday, she was expected to select a husband. It was to be the most important decision of her young life. By tradition the choice of husband was hers. But by law a husband did have to be selected. Only after she was married could she claim the throne as the rightful ruler of Solandia.

Thus, nearly sixteen years after her birth, the great question in Solandia was: Who among her many young suitors would Princess Babette choose to marry? The entire court became a beehive of curiosity. Every move Babette made, everything she said, every man she met was watched and talked about. Only one thing was generally agreed upon: for a princess as beautiful as Babette, only the most handsome man would do.

Shortly before her sixteenth birthday, the prime minister invited Babette's most favored suitors to join her for a week of festivities. He wanted to provide a place for Babette to make her crucial decision away from the distractions of a court caught up in a frenzy of speculation, so he chose the farthest corner of Solandia—the Northern Forest.

The prime minister spoke these final words to Babette before she left in her carriage: "Choose well, my princess. Remember, the eyes of history will be looking at you."

The weather was lovely. Skies were cobalt blue by day, star bright and crisp by night. In short, each day was perfect. "Like Babette," one of the handsome young men noted as he glanced lovingly (so all could see him do so) at a portrait of Babette with which each suitor had been provided.

Babette, meanwhile, met first with this young man and then another young man. She gossiped idly with one, talked philosophy with another. With a third she went walking. With yet another she went running. Sometimes she did a little of each with still another.

For the last day it was agreed that the entire party would hike through the forest, then return to waiting coaches. At that point Babette would announce her choice of a husband. This lucky man would escort her home. Everyone agreed it would be wonderfully romantic and picturesque.

With soldiers to guard them against any mishaps, the party worked their way into the most isolated part of the forest. Once there, the royal trail master announced it was time to go back to the coaches. A tremor of excitement passed through the crowd. Babette was about to make her decision.

At that moment Babette, remembering the prime minister's stern admonition to make her choice with care, called to the royal trail master and said, "I need to have a few moments of privacy to make my decision."

"Perhaps it would be best for me to stay," the trail master said.

"No, no," Babette replied. "I require only a short time. I can catch up easily."

Following orders, the trail master waved everybody on while Babette remained. Once alone she clasped her hands and closed her eyes, then began to think very hard about the crucial decision she was about to make.

In the middle of her meditation she heard someone's footsteps. Indignant, Babette opened her eyes.

Not far off stood an old woman staring fixedly at her. The woman's body was thin and twisted. Her face was haggard. Her hair was gray. Her hands were gnarled and ribboned with veins. A tattered shawl of blue and green lay upon her frail shoulders. Babette thought her very ugly.

After a moment of alarm, Babette regained her composure and said, "Who are you? And what are you doing here?"

To which the woman responded, "Who are you to speak so rudely to me?"

"I am Babette, royal princess of Solandia."

"Are you?"

"Can you not tell just by looking at me?" Babette returned, annoyed with the brashness of the woman.

"Perhaps you are what you say," the old woman

said, "but perhaps you are not. I cannot tell because I can't *see* you."

"What nonsense!" Babette replied. "You are talking to *me*. I am talking to *you*."

"I certainly hear you," the woman said, "but all I see is a suit, gloves, a hat, and boots. I don't see a *person*."

"Are you so blind that you don't see my *face*?"

"I assure you, I'm not blind, but I don't see your face."

"But it's right there!" Babette cried, pulling off one of her gloves and touching a finger to her own nose. "What do you think *this* is?"

"It's nothing," the woman exclaimed. "What's more, you have no hand either. Are you, perhaps, a ghost?"

"I am the royal princess of Solandia!" Babette cried, stamping her foot with vexation.

At that moment the royal trail master, concerned that Babette was overdue, had come back with soldiers to check. When he saw the princess talking to someone, he stopped.

Out of the corner of her eye Babette saw the trail master and soldiers approach. Nonetheless, she continued to give most of her attention to the woman.

"Are you aware," Babette informed the old woman, "that you have insulted me?"

"I beg your pardon," the old woman said. "I can only tell you what I see or—in this case—do not see."

"I want this woman arrested!" Babette demanded. "She has insulted me grossly!"

It was a moment's work for the soldiers to take the old woman into custody.

"Take her to the castle prison!" Babette commanded.

That, too, was done, and in moments the royal trail master and Babette were alone.

"Did the old woman hurt you, Princess?"

Babette was about to say no. Instead she said, "Do I look as if I've been hurt?"

The royal trail master studied her carefully.

"No," he said, "not as far as I can see."

"What about my face?"

"To me," he replied, "you look just as you have always looked."

"And what way is that?"

"Without a blemish. Perfect."

"Fine," Babette said. "What you say proves the woman is mad. We've probably saved her from harming herself. I feel better already. Let's catch up with the others."

When Babette reached the carriage, her suitors were all lined up ready for her great decision. Babette, however, could not free her mind from what had just occurred.

"I need a little more time," she announced.

Babette was soon alone in her carriage and going home. Instead of deciding about her suitors, however, she kept thinking about what had happened in the forest. She did not, of course, believe what the old woman had said. Yet she could not get the incident out of her mind.

When Babette arrived at the castle, the prime minister hurried to meet her. "Princess, I understand you met with some trouble in the forest."

"Just some old woman who insulted me."

"Ah, Princess, the world is full of people who do not see things the way they should."

"It was nothing," Babette assured the prime minister. Then she asked, "What happened to her?"

"She's in the palace prison awaiting trial."

"Good," Babette said.

"And you," the prime minister inquired anxiously, "have you made up your mind about your future husband?"

To which Babette replied, "I was distracted. I could not see my way clear. I will make my decision tonight."

That night, however, as Babette was preparing for bed, she examined her face in one of the portraits she used as a mirror. Turning to a lady-in-waiting, she asked, "Tell me, what do I look like?"

To this the woman replied, "Why, Princess, you look exactly like your portrait."

"Which one?"

"Your favorite one. The one on your vanity table."

Babette had a restless sleep. In the morning the prime minister again came to ask if she had chosen her husband.

"Never mind all that," Babette replied. "Has that woman I met in the forest been punished yet?"

"Her trial is today. I assure you it's only a formality. She will be banished and you'll never have to set eyes on her ugliness again. You're not worried about her, are you?"

"No," Babette replied. "But she did only insult me. Perhaps she feels bad about that. If she would apologize and admit her mistake, I might be inclined to forgive her."

"How gracious of you," the prime minister said. "And the matter of your husband . . . ?"

"Soon."

That afternoon Babette was seated in her audience chamber when the old woman was ushered into her presence between two soldiers. Her feet were in chains so she could not run away. Her hands were tied behind her back. As she approached the throne she lifted her eyes and gazed at Babette intently.

"What is your name?" Babette asked.

"Esmeralda."

"Very well, Esmeralda," Babette said, "when you look upon me *now* what do you see?"

"Your clothes," Esmeralda said.

"No more?"

"If I speak the truth you'll punish me again."

"Take off her chains. Undo her hands," Babette commanded.

It was done.

"Now," Babette said to Esmeralda, "you are a free woman. Tell me what you see."

"I see nothing."

"That's impossible!" Babette cried.

"Princess, I cannot see what I cannot see."

"But everybody else sees me!" Babette retorted.

Esmeralda shook her head. "The truth is, Princess," she said, "you are invisible."

"Invisible! What nonsense!"

"What would you say if I could prove it to you?" Esmeralda asked.

"You can't!"

"Very well. I request that a mirror be brought here."

"A what?" asked a puzzled Babette.

"A mirror."

"What is a mirror?"

"It's a device for seeing the truth about yourself."

"More nonsense!" Babette cried with indignation. "It's impossible to see oneself."

To which Esmeralda said, "How else can you know who you are?"

Babette laughed at the old woman's foolishness. "Look about the walls. What do you see?"

Esmeralda gazed at all the portraits of Babette that hung about. Then she said, "I see one false face in many different poses."

"You are mocking me!" Babette cried. "To know what I look like I need only look at my portraits. They are art and the whole world knows art *always* tells the truth. Those faces are *me*."

Esmeralda looked from the portraits to Babette and back again. "That may be," she said, "but I can't see it."

"Go back to jail!" Babette cried, and Esmeralda was led away.

Left alone, Babette was greatly agitated. She paced and fretted, then sent for the prime minister.

"Your highness," he said, "have you—"

Babette interrupted. "Are there such things called mirrors, devices by which one can see one-self?"

"My princess," the prime minister said soothingly, "a mirror is an antique device. Very primitive. It was your own wise mother who banished them from the queendom. Here in Solandia, we are civilized. We live by the arts."

"Fetch me a mirror!" Babette demanded.

The prime minister tried to resist. "Are you dissatisfied by your portraits? Would you like a new one painted? We have some wonderful new young artists who can paint whatever you'd like. Besides, the whole queendom is waiting—"

"Fetch me a mirror!"

The prime minister sighed. "I suppose there's one in the attic of the Royal Museum, but—"

"Get it!"

After a long search, an old mirror—hardly bigger than her own hand, and covered by a cloth—was brought to Princess Babette.

Babette gave the mirror to the prime minister first. "Look at it," she commanded, "and tell me what you see."

Nervously, the prime minister did as he'd been ordered to do.

"Well, what do you see?"

"A very old man."

Then Babette gave the mirror to a lady-in-waiting. "What do *you* see?"

"A nervous woman."

She gave it to a guard. "And you?"

"A frightened soldier."

"Leave me alone!" Babette cried. It was done. Then she took the mirror and propped it before her on her vanity table. With very great care she combed her hair, patted her cheeks, pouted her lips, then lifted her chin ever so slightly. That was the way her favorite portrait showed her. Then Babette reached out and—heart pounding—looked at the mirror.

When Babette saw *nothing*, she gave a shriek and collapsed upon the floor.

For the rest of the day Babette refused to see anyone. Instead she spent hours sitting before the small mirror, staring at her nothingness. How painful it was to admit that she was invisible, which meant that not only could no one truly see her but also that they had *never* seen her. Far better to tell herself that she was dreaming, ill, or even mad. Had not her mother gone mad? In her heart, though, Babette knew she was not mad.

Before Babette was willing to fully admit the truth—that the old woman was right, she was invisible—she decided upon another test. First she took down all her portraits from the wall. Then she sent for the prime minister.

"Princess," he said, "the entire queendom is waiting for—"

"Prime minister," she said, "look at me."

"With pleasure."

"What do you see?" she asked.

As he normally did, the prime minister stole a hasty glance at the walls where the portraits of Princess Babette usually hung. When he saw that they were gone, he frowned, placed a hand over his eyes, and said, "Princess, I've a frightful headache."

"I insist!" Babette cried. "Tell me what I look like!"

"I don't know," he admitted.

"Go away from me," Babette cried, "and send that woman, Esmeralda, to me."

"She's gone."

"Gone!"

"At her trial—for her unspeakable rudeness to you—the judge banished her."

"Where?"

"Where you found her. The remote Northern Forest."

"But . . . !"

"She did, however, leave you a note."

"Send for it!"

The prime minister hurried away, and though he himself did not return, he had Esmeralda's note slipped underneath Babette's door. It read:

> *Babette: If you wish to become visible, you must first find yourself in a mirror, then take for yourself what is wanted.*
>
> *Esmeralda*

Babette read the letter three times but could make no sense of it. Raging with frustration, she tore the letter into shreds. For a while she was too agitated to do anything but prowl about her room, pausing now and again to steal glances at the small mirror. When she continued to see nothing, she moaned, then paced some more.

Every once in a while there came a knocking on the door. It would be a lady-in-waiting or some other member of the court asking permission to enter, to help her, to feed her, to conduct some business. Babette refused them all.

When she could no longer deny her own hunger, she requested food, but she also requested a box of paints. When it was all delivered, she forgot about eating. Instead she sat before her mirror and with a brush, painted her face.

First she painted the outlines of her face, then her eyes, nose, and a mouth. She could see what she painted in the mirror, but since Babette was no artist, the result was very crude.

"I shall take art lessons," Babette told herself, "or pay artists to paint me every day."

The thought made her sad. The sadness brought tears that trickled down her cheeks, leaving tracks of emptiness. She tried to smooth in the spots. Her face became a smudge.

Babette picked up one of the portraits that she

had removed from the walls. With scissors she cut out the canvas face, punched out holes for her eyes, then attached string to the mask she had made. That done, she placed the image over her face.

This time when she looked in the mirror she saw herself as she had always looked before. The canvas mask, however, was hot and sticky. What's more, she could not eat or scratch her nose. It was hard to breathe. Stymied to the point of fury, Babette tore off the mask and tossed it away.

That night Babette lay upon her bed, weeping and bewailing her fate. How she wished she had never met Esmeralda! But thinking of the old woman made her recall the message that had been left.

If you wish to become visible, you must first find yourself in a mirror, then take for yourself what is wanted.

"Ah," Babette sighed to herself, "if only I knew how! If only I could find Esmeralda to ask her." The next moment she recalled that the old woman had been banished to the Northern Forest.

Right then Babette resolved to find her.

It was at about two in the morning when Princess Babette slipped silently down to the castle stables, saddled a fast horse, and set off at a gallop.

Dawn had just arrived when Babette reached the Northern Forest, where she had first met Esmeralda. All was still. The earth seemed to sigh. Babette's horse blew a frosty breath and nervously pawed the ground.

In the not-too-far distance Babette observed a glow. At first she thought it was the sun. But when it did not move, Babette decided to investigate. She slipped off her horse and began to walk beneath the great canopy of trees. A chill wind blew into her face. The only sound was her soft tread upon the ground.

The closer she moved to the glow, the brighter it became. Now and again sparks of light exploded as if from a spinning diamond. Soon a cold, white, and luminescent mist began to flow among the fingerlike roots of trees. The mist seemed to be coming from the direction of the glow.

Babette stepped into the mist. It eddied about her ankles like a mountain stream. She walked through it, moving in the direction from which it flowed. The farther she went, the brighter the glow ahead grew.

Then, at last, she saw what was causing the glow. Suspended between two great tree trunks was a gigantic mirror. It was taller than it was wide—like a door—and framed by wood that had been intricately carved. These carvings were of forest animals and birds, as well as flowers, all crafted so well they seemed to be alive. The mirror's surface shimmered and sparkled and reflected the forest that surrounded it.

Though the mirror appeared to be solid, at the bottom its substance came forth in an ever-flowing fountain of glowing white mist. It was the same mist that ran through the trees and that Babette had followed.

Babette approached the mirror cautiously. When she stood before it, she looked at herself. What she saw was the clothing she wore but, as before, nothing of her face or hands. Yet the more she looked at the mirror, the more she saw what appeared to be a multitude of shadowy faces within the mirror itself. There were hundreds, thousands of these faces, none

66

distinct, all drifting like feathers in a gentle wind.

She reached out toward the mirror. Instead of feeling a hard surface, her fingers passed into the mirror itself. Alarmed, she withdrew her hand. But then she touched the mirror again, pressing at it until her arm went in up to her elbow. It was as if the mirror—or what she thought was the mirror—was in fact a doorway.

She placed her other hand against the glass. It, too, went through. For a moment she just stood there, arms extended into the mirror. Then, with her heart pounding, she stepped inside.

Babette found herself in a large room suffused with a dusty light, the source of which she could not determine. The room contained nothing but mirrored doors complete with hinges and handles. These doors were everywhere, on the walls, the ceiling, the floor, so many it was impossible to count them. None were marked, nor was there any indication of what lay behind any of them.

Babette stood in the center of the room and gazed about. Every movement she made was reflected in all the mirrored doors. It was as if

67

she were in the very middle of a kaleidoscope.

"Hello!" she cried. There was no answer.

Increasingly frightened, feeling as though she had entered a trap, Babette wanted to get out. She reached toward the door she thought she had used to enter the room. It swung open slowly.

Beyond was another room. Babette looked in. The room was full of eyes, millions of them. Each one was a different color, a different shape. Some seemed sad. Others were bright and cheerful. A few blinked. Others stared. Some appeared brave; others were evasive. A few of the eyes stared fixedly at her, while some, as if shy, shifted away.

Babette reached out and touched one of the eyes. It blinked and fell into her hand. From her palm it stared up at her. Babette stared back. As she did she remembered the message from Esmeralda,

If you wish to become visible, you must first find yourself in a mirror, then take for yourself what is wanted.

Hand trembling, Babette carried the eye to her face

68

and pressed it in. She took away her hand. The eye stayed.

Slowly, not yet sure what she was doing, Babette reached out for yet another eye, then pressed that, too, to her face.

Now she turned and stepped out of the room, back into the central hall. She gazed about. In countless images she saw her new eyes. But when she looked back at the doorway through which she had just come, the room of eyes had vanished.

Babette, beginning to understand, went to another door and pulled it open. It was a roomful of thumbs. Like the room of eyes, they were of all kinds, shapes, colors, sizes. She reached for one and pulled it on her right hand like a glove finger. Then she held the thumb before her eyes—and saw it. With growing excitement Babette reached for another thumb—only to realize that it was also for a right hand. She had to make sure to get a left one. After looking about she found one, and slipped it on.

From then on Babette went from room to room, finding that each contained something different: here ears, there elbows. Ankles in this one. Noses in

another. Bit by bit she picked and chose, taking more and more time than she had at first.

When she had finished there was only one door remaining. What could she have forgotten? She turned the knob and the door opened onto the forest. She stepped out, then turned back toward the great mirror. For the first time Babette saw herself as she was: complete.

What she saw was not perfect. Her left foot was slightly bigger than her right. One earlobe had a crease, the other did not. Her face was not quite symmetrical. What's more, she realized that in her first haste she had selected one blue eye and one brown eye. But—she reminded herself—it did not matter. They were *her* eyes and they could see themselves.

Did Babette marry? Did she become queen? Did she live happily ever after? No one knows. All that *is* known is that from that time on, Babette could see herself.

SIMON

There was a boy, Simon by name, who was born into a family of the most modest means. Nonetheless, he was a healthy, handsome baby, given to all the joys and pleasures of babyhood.

An only child, Simon was indulged by both his mother and father to such a degree that he grew up to be someone who always assumed he was the center of attention. In fact, as Simon grew older he found that he could charm anyone with his bright looks and sharp wit. And though he always managed to avoid doing anything that might be of help or use to his parents, he was quite comfortable in demanding and taking his fill of food, clothing, or pleasure. No matter that there was little money; no wish or whim of Simon's went unanswered.

One of the things Simon asked for and received was a rifle. From the moment he first had the gun in his hands, Simon's chief desire was to become known as the best marksman in the land.

As Simon grew into a young man, his demands continued to grow. Nothing but the finest would satisfy him. Hardly a surprise then that he came to believe that people could do no better than admire him. To the question "What do you want to do with your life?" he was quick to reply, "I intend to have the whole world gaze upon me with admiration and envy."

Over the years Simon's parents grew poorer. Though they had given as much as they could to their son, there came a time when they could no longer satisfy him. This made Simon very angry.

"You are an unappreciative family," he told them. "For I, who am the best in the world, can be content only with the best."

To this his father replied, "Simon, for all I know, what you say may be true. But as you see, we have nothing left to give."

To this his mother added, "Your wants and demands have quite ruined us. If you desire more, you must get it elsewhere, and you must get it for yourself."

At these words Simon picked up his rifle, turned his back upon his parents, and left home without so much as a farewell. It made his mother and father weep to see him go.

Simon journeyed to another village that was near a great forest. Since this forest was famous for the wild animals that lived in it, he decided to become a hunter. By selling what he killed, he was sure he could earn enough money for his wants.

All Simon's energies now turned to hunting. He was very good at it. It did not take long before the sound of him coming through the forest was enough to bring terror to all the four-footed creatures who lived there. They knew that Simon was an excellent shot, that he had no mercy, and that he was greedy.

One day, when Simon brought his slaughter to the

marketplace, a merchant took him aside.

"Simon," the merchant said, "you do very well in what you bring me. But let me tell you, as great as is the demand for furs and hides, these days what the rich want more than anything are *feathers*. Mind you," the merchant warned, "not ordinary feathers, but gloriously colored ones. The kind you can only find in the deepest parts of the forest. A good shot like you should have no trouble with that.

"Simon, bring me such feathers and you shall become rich!"

These words were enough for Simon. Rifle in hand, he set off into the forest and began hunting birds. With great cunning he shot hundreds of them, stripped them of their feathers, and left their carcasses to rot. As for the feathers, he sold them to the merchant.

Just as the merchant had promised, Simon soon grew rich and well known in the region. But he was not satisfied. Still desiring that the whole world look upon him with awe, he hunted even more.

As Simon brought in more and more wonderful feathers, the demand for them actually grew. Not only were greater quantities wanted but there were also higher prices for the most unusual kinds. To meet this demand, Simon went deeper and deeper into the forest in search of the new and strange.

One day at the market the merchant said, "Simon, my friend, it is believed that in the most remote part of the forest lives the Queen-of-All-the-Birds. Her feathers—so I've heard—have the look, the feel, even the taste of pure gold.

"Fetch me *her* feathers and you shall be the wealthiest of men. The entire world shall sit up and take notice of you."

His head bursting with visions of glory, Simon set off in pursuit of the Golden Bird, traveling where few hunters had been before. Everywhere he went he shot great numbers of birds. But as for the Golden Bird, she never passed before his eyes. All the same, Simon kept searching.

One day Simon found himself in the darkest, most tangled part of the forest. As he stood looking about, his hunting bag full of feathers, he caught sight of what looked like gold fluttering among the trees. Not sure at first if he was seeing correctly, he approached the glitter stealthily.

At last he drew close enough to see the bird. In the rays of the sun that filtered down among the many-fingered branches, this bird's wings sparkled brighter than the sun itself. Her beak was blue, sharp, and precise. Her feet were crimson red. Most splendid of all was a crown of jet black upon her head.

The moment Simon saw her he was certain she was the Queen-of-All-the-Birds, the Golden Bird herself. Instantly, his mind filled with dazzling images of the money and fame he was sure to get after he killed her and stripped her of her feathers.

With his loaded rifle in hand, Simon inched forward. The bird did not seem to notice. She even fluttered down to a closer branch.

Ever deliberate and sly, Simon crept to within a few feet of the bird. Without a sound he lifted his rifle and took precise aim at her breast.

Just as he was about to squeeze the trigger, the bird turned to him and quite calmly said, "Why do you want to shoot me, Simon?"

Simon, never taking the Golden Bird from his gun

sights, said, "Because I need your feathers."

"You don't *need* them," the bird replied. "Besides, they are not yours to have."

To this Simon said, "The world is there for me to take. And when I take what I want, everybody shall take notice of me."

"Everybody?" the bird asked.

"Everybody," Simon insisted.

"Then," the bird replied, "I shall help you achieve exactly that." With a sudden flutter of her great wings, she sprang upon Simon.

Even as she did, Simon pulled the trigger. The gun fired. His aim was accurate. The bullet hit true, piercing the Golden Bird's heart. All the same she had sufficient strength in her leap to reach him. As she tumbled down, one wing brushed over his face and neck. Then she fell before his feet.

As the Golden Bird fell, all the leaves from the trees fell, too, making the sound of soft rain. Then the forest grew absolutely still, becoming as silent as a cloudless sky, heavy as the whole earth, thick as the deepest sea.

Startled, Simon looked up. Hundreds of birds

were sitting on the now leafless branches, gazing mutely at him and the Golden Bird, which lay on the ground before his feet.

At first, Simon merely gazed back. When the birds did nothing, he shrugged, snatched up the dead Golden Bird by the neck, and stuffed her into his hunting bag.

Turning his back on the silent, watching birds, Simon started off. Already his mind was trying to calculate how much he should ask for the golden feathers. He decided to demand millions.

As Simon walked through the forest, he began to hear high-pitched sounds. At first he paid them no mind. But as the sounds continued, he realized that his name was being called. "Simon! Simon! Simon!"

Simon stopped. He looked about in search of the people who were calling his name. He saw no one. But the hundreds of birds that had been there before were following him.

Nervous now, Simon continued on. Once more he heard his name being called. "Simon! Simon!" This time the words came from directly overhead.

He stopped and looked up. The many birds he

had seen before were gone. Now—barely four feet above him—three black ravens had come to rest upon the branches of a dead tree. Their bright beady eyes, like burning black candles, were focused on Simon.

"Is it a bird or a man?" he heard one of the ravens whisper. The first raven's voice was thick and ragged.

"Ask it," the second raven suggested.

Simon, puzzled that he could understand what the birds were saying to one another, stayed to listen.

The third raven hopped along the leafless branch until it dipped and pointed like an accusing finger, just a few inches from Simon's face.

Cocking its head now this way and now that, the third raven croaked, "What are you, Simon, bird or man?"

Simon replied, "I am a man, of course."

"And yet," said the first raven, "you speak to us."

To which the second raven added, "What is more, Simon, your neck is like the neck of a bird."

"For *that* matter," the third raven concluded, "so is your head."

Taken aback, Simon put a hand to his neck. To his

face. It was as the ravens had said. From his neck up he was all *feathers*! What's more, that neck, which had grown in length and was somewhat coiled, supported an oval-shaped head.

Simon felt his eyes. They were perfectly round and set on either side of his face. Where his nose and mouth had been, he felt a long pointed beak. But when he looked down at himself, the rest of his body remained as it had been, like a man's.

Frightened, Simon dropped his rifle and sack and tried to rub away the feathers.

"What a rude fellow you are!" screamed one of the ravens. "We say you are a bird and no more a man than we are. Snobbish creature!"

With a chorus of hoarse cackles, the ravens fell upon Simon, pulling and clawing at him. So fierce was the attack that Simon ran blindly into the forest as fast as he could go. But the ravens followed until Simon managed to push his way into a thick thorny underbrush that was too tangled for even the ravens to follow.

Though badly scratched, Simon did not care because the ravens could not reach him. After a

while, they flew away. As they went, Simon heard them calling his name. It sounded as if they were laughing.

Simon crawled from his hiding place. He had run in fear and had no idea where he was. Now he began to search for a way out of the forest. It did not take long for him to realize he was lost. For the rest of the day and far into the night, Simon wandered help-lessly.

Late that night, by the light of a full moon, he came upon a pool of water. Very thirsty, he paused and bent down. Upon the surface of the pool, mirror-like, he saw an image of himself. From his neck up— wherever the Golden Bird had touched him with her wing—he had turned into a bird.

For a long while Simon stared at his image. At first he tried to tell himself that this was all a dream, that surely he would wake up and be what he had always been. But even as he tried to convince him-self of this, a pack of hunting dogs, howling and bay-ing, leaped out of the bushes and attacked him.

To protect himself, Simon sprang onto a large boulder. There the dogs—baying, snapping, growling—could not touch him. But at the same time, he was trapped.

Simon was still standing on the rock, high above the dogs, trying to find a way to escape, when a group of hunters appeared. They all carried rifles. When the hunters saw Simon atop the rock, they stopped short, amazed by his appearance.

After a moment one of the hunters lifted his gun and was about to fire, when Simon called, "Don't shoot!"

If the hunters had been amazed at the sight of Simon, they were even more astonished that the strange creature could talk.

One of them called out, "Are you man or bird?"

"I am a man!" insisted Simon, relieved to know that though he had understood the talk of birds, he could still speak human language.

"Friend or enemy?" called another of the hunters.

"Friend of all!" Simon pleaded. From somewhere he thought he heard the cackle of the ravens.

"Then lift your hands, or wings, or whatever they are," one of the hunters called, "and come down here."

When the dogs were called off, Simon climbed down from the rock and approached the hunters. When he did he saw that among them was a man with a crown on his head. He was the leader of the band, and a prince.

"Who are you?" asked the prince.

"I am Simon."

"Well, then *what* are you?" the prince questioned, all the while staring with amazement at Simon.

"Through no fault of mine," Simon nervously explained, "magic has turned me into what you see."

"I know nothing of magic," said the prince. "But I do know you are a most curious spectacle! You will come with me. There are others who would enjoy the sight of you."

Simon objected, but the prince would hear no refusal.

Suddenly fearful of what might happen to him, Simon turned and tried to run away. But two of the hunters sprang after him, caught him with ease, and held him tightly. They tied Simon's hands behind his back and placed a rope around his neck. By holding this rope, they were able to take him through the woods. The prince led the way.

Simon, both shocked and hurt to be so badly treated, kept demanding to be set free. The men who held him took no interest in what he said. Quite the contrary. Though they kept gawking at him and talking about him, the men acted as if Simon were incapable of understanding them.

Once, twice, Simon tried to pull upon the rope that held him. All he got for his efforts was a sharp, painful yank back. He had to go along.

After a long march the hunters came to their camp. Many people were there, men and women of the court. Many were dressed in furs and feathers that Simon recognized as adornments he had supplied.

With great excitement the courtiers gathered around Simon, looked at him, poked him, and in general treated him as if he were no more than a dumb beast, marvel though he was.

Enraged, Simon cursed them all. This made the people laugh and tease him more, for they found him to be very funny. At last, for the sake of his own pride, Simon decided to say nothing.

When it was time to eat a great feast was served to all the members of the court. Simon, still tied up, could do nothing more than watch. No one seemed to consider that he might like to join them. True, from time to time people at the prince's table threw him bits of food. Simon, who naturally was used to eating only at a table, at first refused to eat from the ground. But when his hunger grew to be too much, he tried to pick up a few pieces when no one was looking.

The rope, however, held him short. He had to stretch his neck forward and peck at the ground. When people noticed, they found his antics amusing. Simon stopped eating.

At the feast the prince announced that his hunt was over. He was certain he would find nothing more wonderful than the rare bird—he meant Simon—he had already caught. Accordingly, he ordered a cage to be built. This was quickly done and Simon was forced inside. It was not a very big cage. Simon could not lie down. He could only sit. This he did, holding his hands upon the bars to keep his balance.

Sometimes, as he realized his predicament, a fury took hold of him. Unable to control himself, he shook the bars. This caused much laughter and finger pointing, which only made Simon angrier. But there was nothing he could do about it.

When the prince's party was ready to move on, the cage, with Simon in it, was loaded upon a cart and pulled along with all the other baggage. Simon, in his cage, was displayed as the paramount trophy.

For three days, the prince and his party traveled. To Simon's great mortification, he was the center of attraction in every town through which they passed. Since they were going from the country to the city, they went through larger and larger places. Bigger and bigger crowds came to stare, to cheer, and to poke fun.

Simon glowered at his tormentors. Secretly he plotted all the things he intended to do to them when he got free.

At last, the traveling party came to the great city where the prince lived. Through large crowds—news of Simon's capture had spread far and wide—he was led in triumph to the palace.

In anticipation of Simon's arrival at the palace, a much more elaborate cage had been built. He was forced into it. Then the cage, with him inside, was drawn into the air and hung like a chandelier in the very center of the court. That way he could be viewed by all throughout the day.

As the days passed Simon grew sullen. He would not talk or respond to anything or anybody. Sometimes people prodded at him, or banged on the cage to get a reaction. Occasionally Simon would lose his temper. That made people laugh. He screamed insults at them. Though at first people were amused, it did not take long for them to take offense. His cage was placed higher and in a corner.

Months went by. Simon had no view of the outside world except through a small window in the palace wall. This window looked out into the sky. The most Simon could see was the change in the weather.

One day in the hall a great banquet was held. From above Simon listened to the talk, the jokes, the songs. Growing restless, he turned to look through the window. Outside, a storm was raging. As Simon snapped at the occasional bit of food that was thrown to him, he thought that at least he was being fed, and was dry and safe inside.

A small bird, a sparrow, flew into the hall to take refuge from the storm. Exhausted, she rested on the window ledge.

The sparrow fluffed out her feathers, shook her head dry, and began to preen her tail. Then she caught sight of Simon sitting in his cage.

Simon, though pretending not to, watched the sparrow.

The bird took a hop closer. "What ghastly weather!" she chirped.

Simon, grateful for a little friendly conversation, replied, "Yes, it looks it."

The sparrow studied Simon with great interest. "Are you a bird?" she finally whispered.

Eager for sympathy, Simon pressed against the bars of his cage, as close to the sparrow as possible. "I was a man," he replied. "But I was turned, partly, into a bird. Now I'm nothing but a creature in a cage for people to stare at and to make fun of."

The sparrow settled down. "How did you come to be the way you are?" she asked.

Simon told the sparrow how he had hunted birds and sold their feathers, and how one day he shot a most unusual bird and . . .

The sparrow rose up, her eyes flashing with anger. "So *you* are the one who shot our Golden Queen!" she cried with shrill fury. "You deserve all the punishment you have. I'd rather be in the storm than with you." So saying, the sparrow turned around and flew out the window.

Simon's only wish was that he, too, could flee into the storm.

Two years went by. The prince, who had once prized Simon as his most curious object, came to be interested in other things. The cage was moved from the central court to a distant room.

As much as Simon hated being looked upon and made fun of, he found isolation worse. Now he had nothing to see but empty walls.

Occasionally the prince would come by and show Simon to a visitor. Simon, desperate for company, would snap his beak and do tricks, anything to keep the visitors a little longer.

The prince was not amused by such foolishness. He called Simon a vain creature and made a point of *not* staying long. His visits grew fewer and fewer.

At length the prince decided that keeping Simon was more trouble than it was worth. He came to Simon's cage and opened the door.

"Come out," said the prince. "No one is interested in looking at you. You're not wanted anymore. You've become common."

An astonished Simon could hardly believe his ears. He thought the prince was simply playing a trick on him and refused to leave. The prince had to have him pulled from the cage and unceremoniously thrown out of the palace.

For the first time in two years, Simon was free. He was elated. But his moment of joy was brief. As he stood against the palace door, trying to think what to do, a group of children found him. They began to make fun and call him names.

In a fury, Simon bent down, picked up a stone, and threw it. His arm was weak. The stone fell short. The children laughed and jeered more.

Simon ran and hid. He began to wish he were back in his cage. At least he was safe there.

As the day wore on Simon began to feel a pain in his stomach that he knew was hunger. With anger and shock, he realized that the prince had put him out without food or money. He had to find something to eat.

As he walked along in search of food, he passed an open-air café. His stomach growling, he stopped and watched people eat their meals.

Someone complained about him. The manager came out and tried to shoo Simon away.

"I only want something to eat," Simon begged.

"Do you think you get food for nothing?" replied the manager. "One has to work for it. Or is your brain as small as most birds'?"

"Please," cried Simon. "It's only that I've not worked in an ordinary way. I've been on exhibition for the prince. I'm willing to do anything for food."

"Ah," said the manager, "you've led a soft life. But I have a kind heart. I'll make you an offer. With that long beak of yours you should be good at picking up bits the way your fellow birds do. People are always leaving crumbs about when they eat. It attracts rats, and I hate rats. Your job can be picking up the crumbs. My place will be clean, and you'll get something to eat."

Simon was revolted by the suggestion. He started to turn away.

"Where else are you going to get food?" asked the manager.

When Simon felt his stomach growl once more, he agreed to take the job.

The manager led Simon into the restaurant through the back way. There he gave him a white apron and placed a silly cap on his head.

"You might as well amuse my patrons," he said. Then he pushed Simon out onto the floor and told him to get busy working. "Don't assume you have this job forever," he warned. "If you don't work hard, out you'll go!"

At first Simon hung back along the walls of the restaurant, pecking only at the crumbs that lay there. The bits of food whetted his appetite. He reached for more and more. The patrons were greatly amused. They began to throw food at him. Simon, unable to resist, gobbled greedily. People laughed.

Within a short time Simon, in order to encourage the patrons and keep his job, began to perform tricks, jokes, and songs, things he had learned from the banquet tables of the prince.

This went over rather well—for a while. It did not take long before the patrons, most of whom came to the café on a regular basis, grew annoyed. They didn't want to hear the same jokes, the same songs. They began to complain to the manager that the bird-man was a distraction. It took only a few complaints before Simon was told to leave. He was no longer wanted.

In despair, Simon left. He had nowhere to go. It was then that he thought of his home. Unable to think of any other place to go, he decided to return to his parents and beg for mercy.

Simon traveled for a week. He went through all the cities and towns through which he had come. This time, however, he traveled by darkest night so he would not be seen. Only when he grew hungry would he emerge into the light of day to do tricks on street corners for bits of bread.

When he came to the edge of his own village, he grew fearful. Ashamed and afraid to show himself there, he waited until it grew dark.

When night came he made his way through back

alleys to his parents' house. Timidly he knocked on the door.

His mother opened it. His father stood behind her. When they saw the strange creature, they were taken aback.

"May we help you?" his mother asked.

"I am your son, Simon."

The two old people looked at the creature on the doorstep with disbelief. Then they became angry.

"Our Simon," said his father, "was the most handsome of young men. He would dress in nothing but the best. But you, your feathers are dirty and you're dressed in rags.

"Anyway, Simon would not come here. This house wasn't good enough for him. He went off to make his fortune, and no doubt has become rich and powerful. No, Simon wouldn't come back here."

"In fact," his mother added, "I suspect that he sent you here to make fun of us!"

So saying, his parents slammed the door.

Heartbroken, exhausted, Simon made his way by cover of night into the forest. When he found a soft place beneath a tree, he lay down. He began to wish that he might never rise again.

Just as he was falling asleep, he heard the baying of hunting dogs. Instantly he remembered how he had been captured before. He had not the slightest desire to be caught again.

To protect himself, he dashed into the woods, running from the sound. Yet no matter where he ran, the baying grew louder. First it was on one side of him, then on the other. He was surrounded.

Certain he was being hunted and that the dogs were closing in, Simon plunged about frantically in search of an escape. Suddenly he caught sight of a golden glimmer springing among the leaves.

He ran forward. There, flitting from branch to branch, was the Golden Bird. In the moonlight he saw her just as he had seen her before—wings aglitter, black crown upon her head, red feet, blue beak sharp and precise.

Simon froze, amazed to see the bird he thought he had killed. He was just about to call out to her when he saw a hunter break from a thicket. The hunter raised his gun to his shoulder and aimed at the Golden Bird.

Instantly, Simon leaped forward, putting himself between bird and hunter just as the hunter pulled the trigger. The gun fired at the Golden Bird. But the bullet struck Simon. He fell instantly.

The hunter, seeing a human form fall and fearing he had killed a man, turned and fled.

As Simon lay upon the ground dying, the forest became utterly still. He opened his eyes and looked up. The trees of the forest were covered with birds, all of whom were staring at him. Among them was the Golden Bird. Simon gazed at her. "Is it really you?" he managed to cry out. "The one I thought I killed?"

The Golden Bird fluttered down by his side. "Yes, it's me," she replied softly. "And you, are you the one whom all the world was to notice?"

"Yes," he whispered.

"And *did* the whole world take notice?"

After a moment Simon said, "Yes, but there was one who never noticed the world."

"Who was that?"

"Me," said Simon and closed his eyes.

Not a leaf in the forest moved. Then the Golden Bird swept her wings over Simon's body. As she did, he was transformed again. He became a bird—a complete bird—of great majesty. With another sweep of her wings, the Golden Bird brought Simon back to life.

Suddenly the Golden Bird leaped into the air. Immediately Simon followed, his great wings beating the dark night. He was flying by her side, whole and free.

Look for All the Unforgettable Stories by Newbery Honor Author

★AVI★

THE TRUE CONFESSIONS OF CHARLOTTE DOYLE
71475-2/ $4.50 US/ $5.99 Can

NOTHING BUT THE TRUTH   71907-X/ $4.50 US/ $5.99 Can

THE MAN WHO WAS POE   71192-3/ $4.50 US/ $5.99 Can

SOMETHING UPSTAIRS   70853-1/ $4.50 US/ $6.50 Can

PUNCH WITH JUDY   72253-4/ $3.99 US/ $4.99 Can

A PLACE CALLED UGLY   72423-5/ $4.50 US/ $5.99 Can

SOMETIMES I THINK I HEAR MY NAME
72424-3/$4.50 US/ $5.99 Can

─────────── And Don't Miss ───────────

ROMEO AND JULIET TOGETHER (AND ALIVE!) AT LAST
70525-7/ $3.99 US/ $4.99 Can

S.O.R. LOSERS   69993-1/ $4.50 US / $5.99 Can

WINDCATCHER   71805-7/ $4.50 US/ $5.99 Can

BLUE HERON   72043-4 / $4.50 US/ $5.99 Can

"WHO WAS THAT MASKED MAN, ANYWAY?"
72113-9 / $3.99 US/ $4.99 Can

POPPY   72769-2 / $4.50 US/ $5.99 Can